To the rescuers,
to each person who helps to protect animals,
to those who foster and adopt,
to the animal humane and animal welfare groups,
and to the animal law advocates,
this book is dedicated with gratitude and admiration.

The Gryphon Press

—a voice for the voiceless—

Special Thanks from Joe Hyatt: to Carolyn Hyatt for giving me every ounce of my artistic ability, and for being my biggest fan; and a very special thank you to my wife, Tania, for inspiring me always to be a better artist and person.

A portion of profits from this book will be donated to shelters and animal rescue societies.

Design by Rachel Holscher
Text set in Cochin by Prism Publication Services
Manufactured in Canada by Friesens Corporation

Library of Congress Control Number: 2006923847

ISBN-10: 0-940719-01-0
ISBN-13: 978-0-940719-01-9

3 5 7 9 10 8 6 4

I am the voice of the voiceless:
Through me, the dumb shall speak;
Till the deaf world's ear be made to hear
The cry of the wordless weak.

—from a poem by Ella Wheeler Wilcox, early 20th-century poet

Buddy Unchained

Daisy Bix • **Joe Hyatt**

The Gryphon Press
—a voice for the voiceless—

Not long ago, I was chosen by a family to live with them.

I have food in my bowl. I have clean water to drink.

Sometimes I get a treat!

They take me for walks.

They play with me.

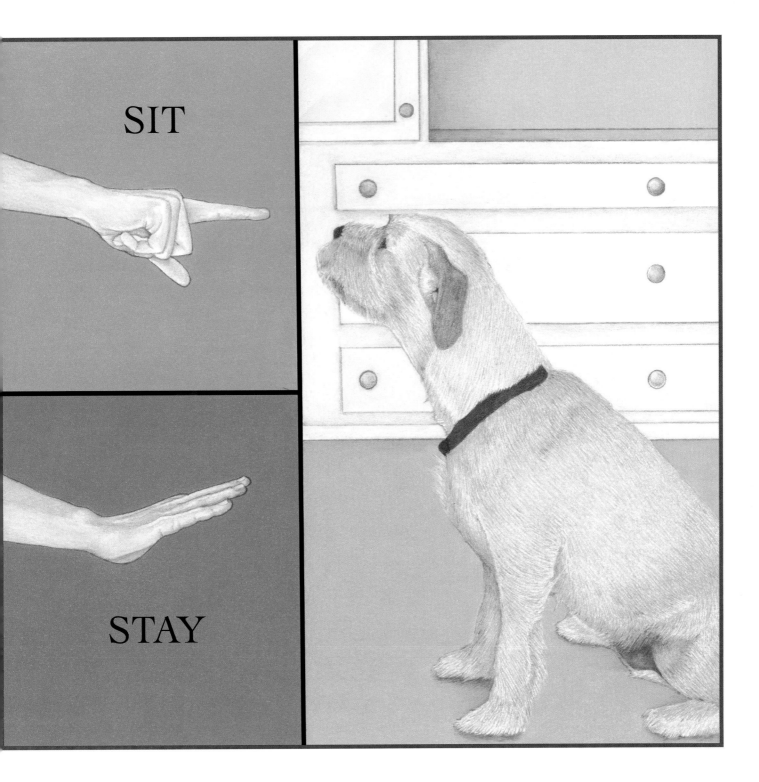

SIT

STAY

They teach me to know what they want from me.

But I used to live in a different place. I slept alone in the garage.

Every day I was put outside. My collar was clipped to a chain.
When it rained, my fur was wet clear through.

Once in awhile, kids threw things at me.
I couldn't protect myself. I don't know why they did that.

When I got twisted in the chain, I couldn't sit down or move
until someone from the house came and untangled it.

Many days those people forgot to change the water in my dish.
It tasted bad. I was so thirsty I drank it anyway.

Sometimes they forgot to feed me. I was hungry most of the time.

When it got very cold, my paws hurt.

One day I was so cold that I lay down and couldn't get up.

A person I didn't know came and took off my chain.

He took me away from that place.

He brought me to a place where they took care of me.

A person carefully clipped my claws.
They were so long I could hardly walk.

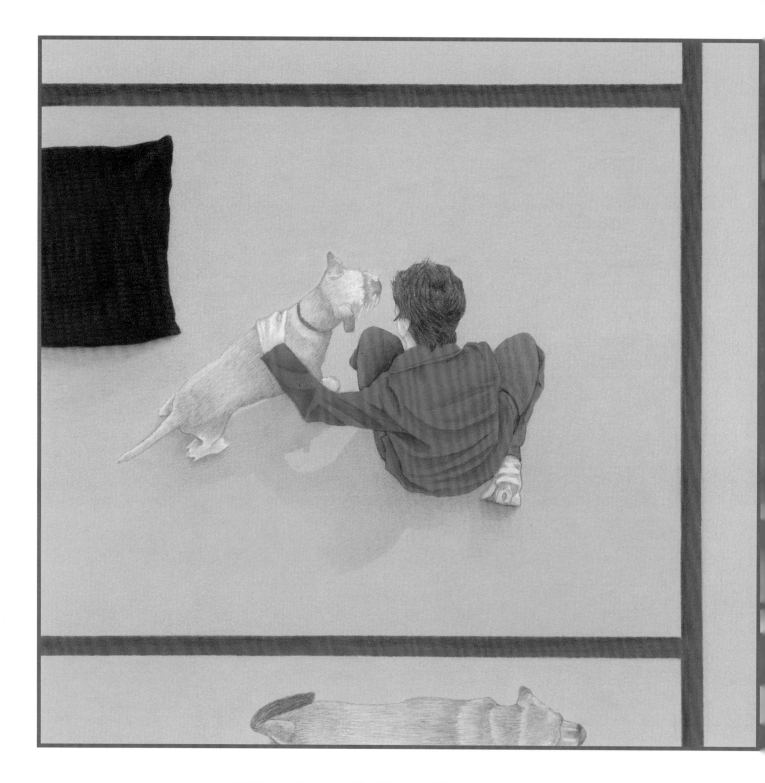

When I was feeling all right again,
they put me into a place with food and water.

The people I live with now came to visit. They chose me to be
part of their family for always. They call me Buddy.

"Good dog, Buddy," they say to me every day.
They give me pats and hugs.

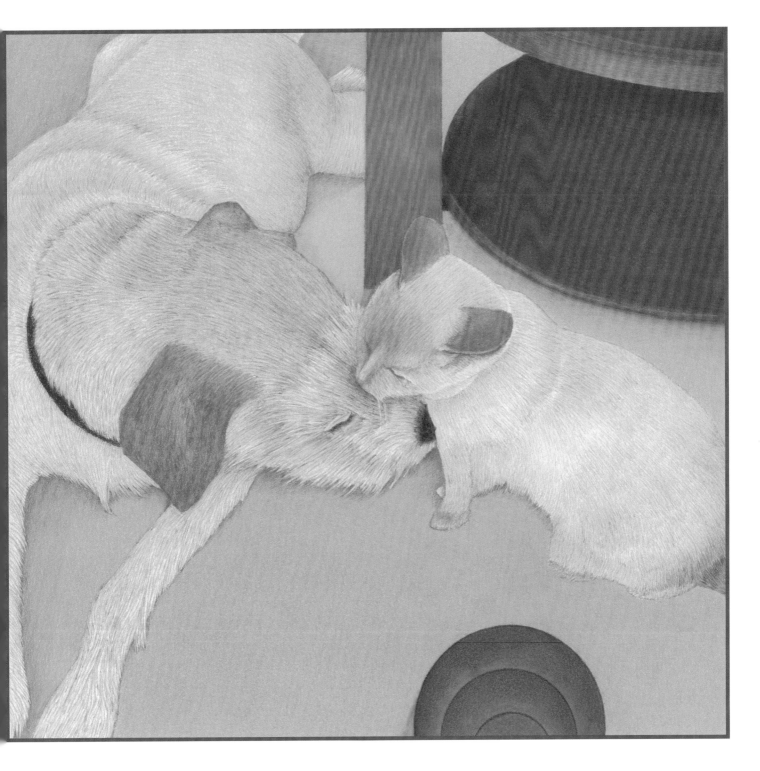

I have friends to play with.

I have my real home. Now I have everything.

Helping Dogs Like Buddy

Dogs and People

A dog offers its person or family unquestioning love, loyalty, and the joy of companionship. In return, a dog requires a caring home, adequate food and water, regular daily walks, and positive interaction with people. A dog should not be left outdoors in bad weather or in dangerous temperatures. If a dog must be left outside at certain times, it should be in an enclosure large enough so that the dog is able to exercise, with shelter from heat and cold, sun and bad weather.

Don't Tether a Dog Outside

A dog chained or roped outside has no companionship, cannot defend itself, and is tethered where it must also drop its wastes. Often dogs kept this way are also neglected, left without proper food or water. Many communities have laws against such neglect. When you see a dog being neglected and abused, don't look away. Take action. Call your local humane society or animal control agency; they know the state laws and can speak to the dog's owner about addressing the problem, or may suggest that the dog be voluntarily surrendered so that it can be given a new and better home.

Resources

To find help and contact information for animal protection groups in your community go to: http://www.Pets911.com.

Other Web sites with useful information include:
Dogs Deserve Better at http://www.dogsdeservebetter.com/home
Unchain Your Dog at http://www.unchainyourdog.org

You can find more information at these sites:
ASPCA's "Fight Cruelty" at http://www.aspca.org/site/
Humane Society of the United States Web site, "What to Do About a Dog Who's Left
    Outside" at http://www.hsus.org"
PETA's "Unchain a Dog" at http://www.HelpingAnimals.com

Give a Dog Like Buddy the Chance for a Happy Ending

If your family has decided to take on the pleasures and responsibilities of a dog, consider fostering or adopting a dog. So many dogs, like Buddy, need a caring home.